ROCKFORD PUBLIC LIBRARY
3 1112 020501132

D1681742

E RUEDA, C
Rueda, Claudia
Hungry bunny

WITHDRAWN
103118

hungry bunny

Claudia Rueda

GRRR

chronicle books · san francisco

Here I come!

GRR

GRRR

Can you hear my tummy rumble?
I'm one hungry bunny!

GRR
GRRR

It's time for a red, delicious, and . . .

hard-to-reach apple.

Maybe you could help!
Could you please

shake

the book so that the
apples fall down?

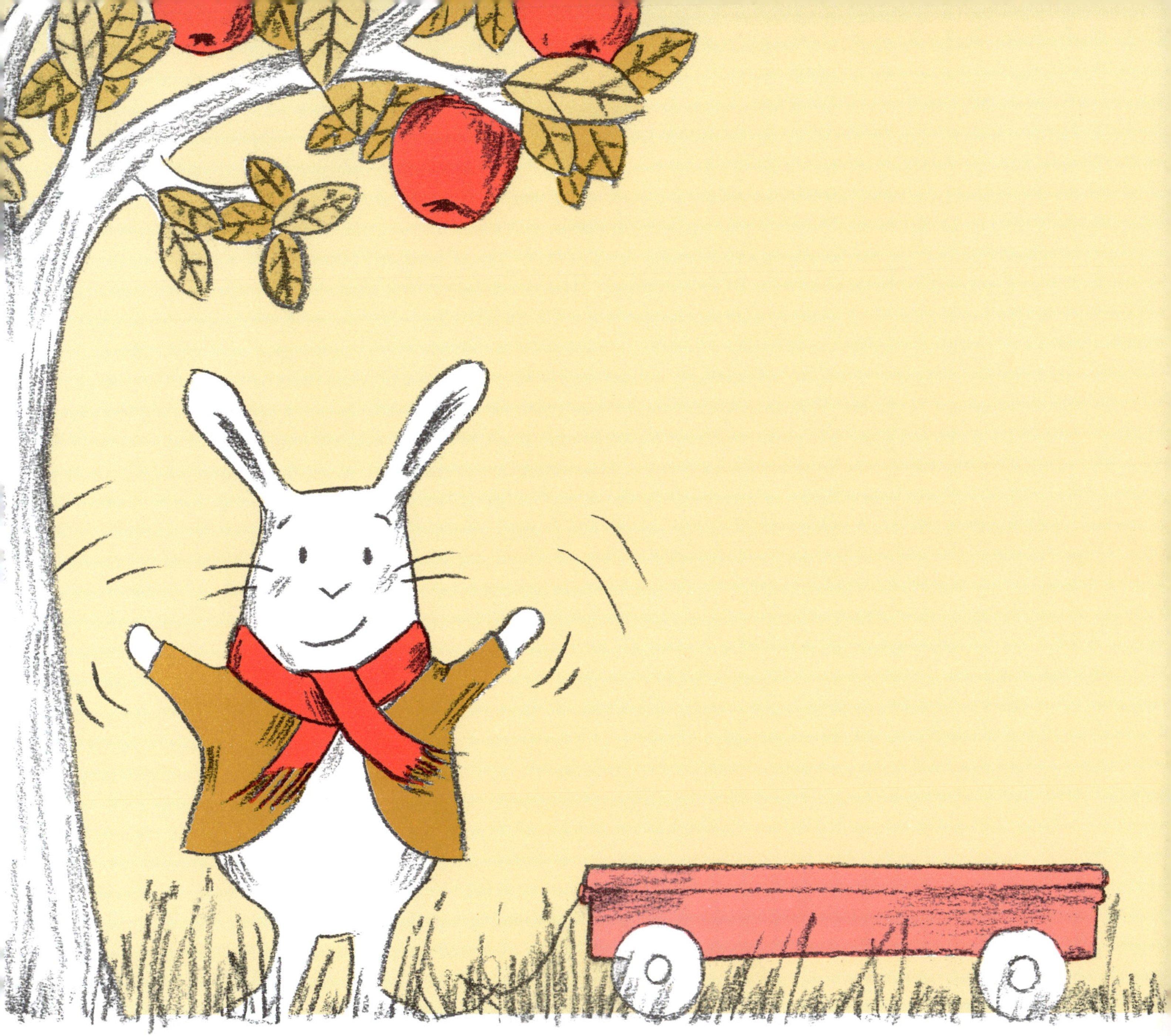

Not the leaves!
Could you

blow

them away?

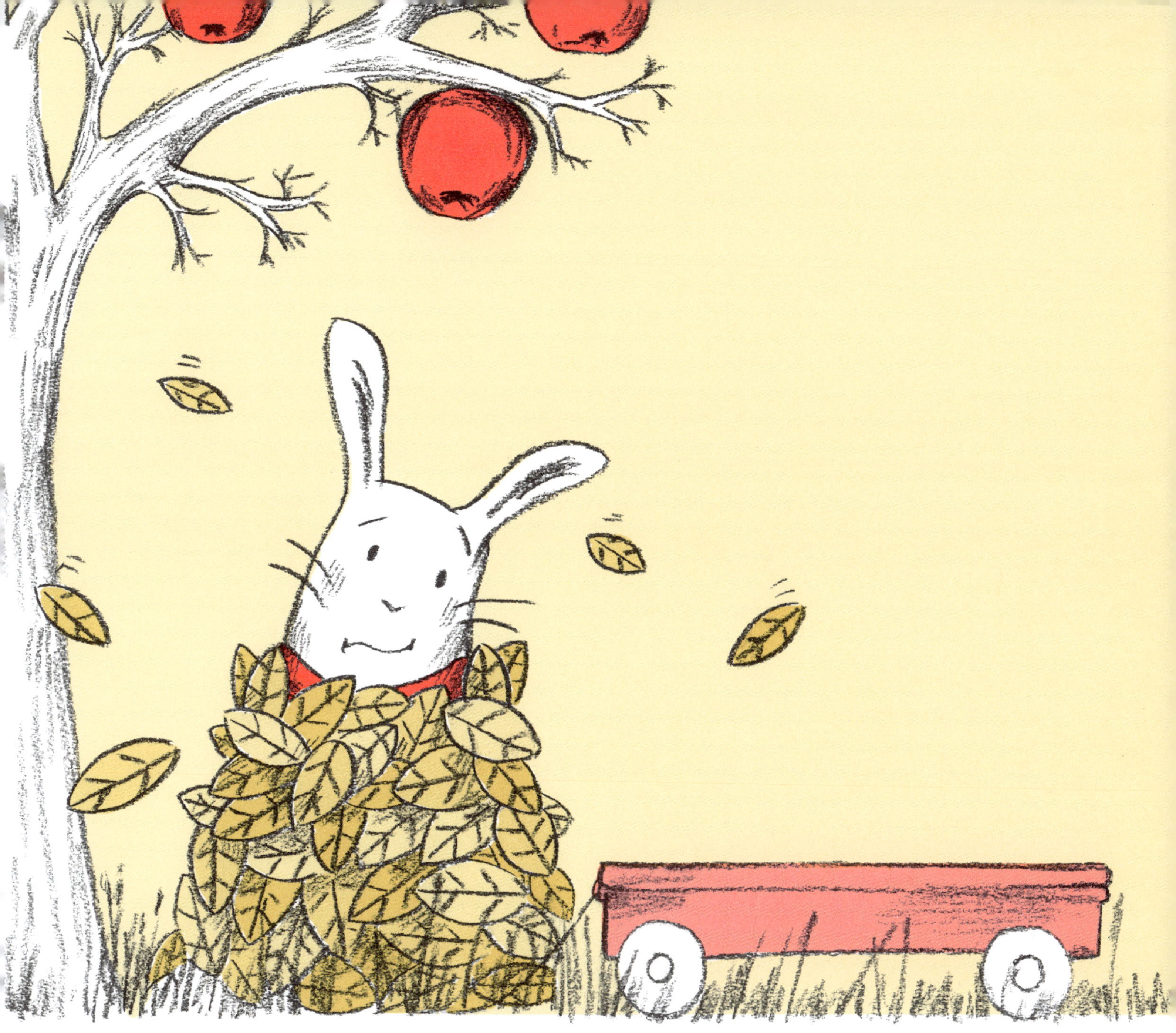

That's much better.
Thank you!

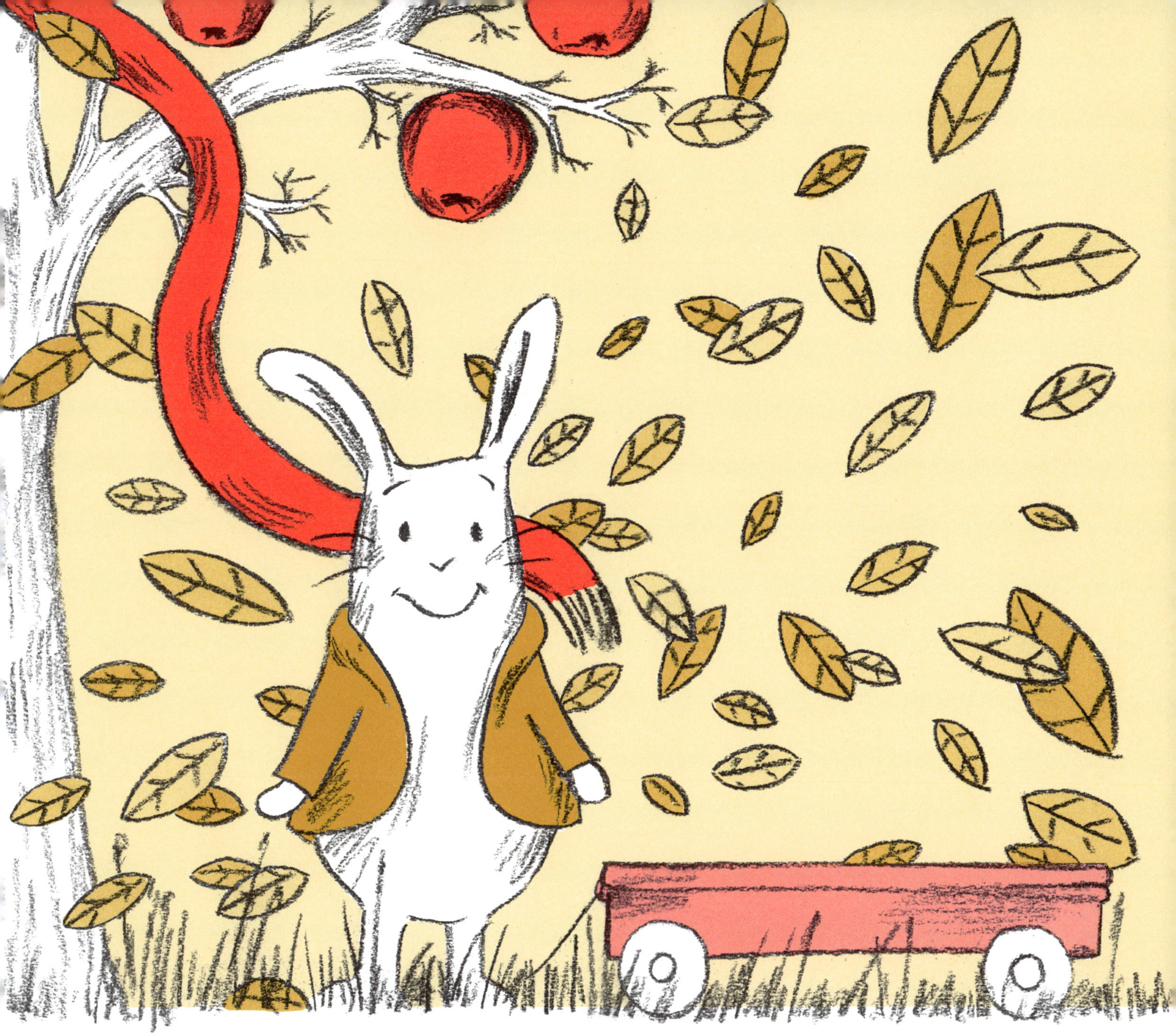

Oh, no!
My scarf has blown away, too!
It's stuck in the book.
And I'm still hungry.

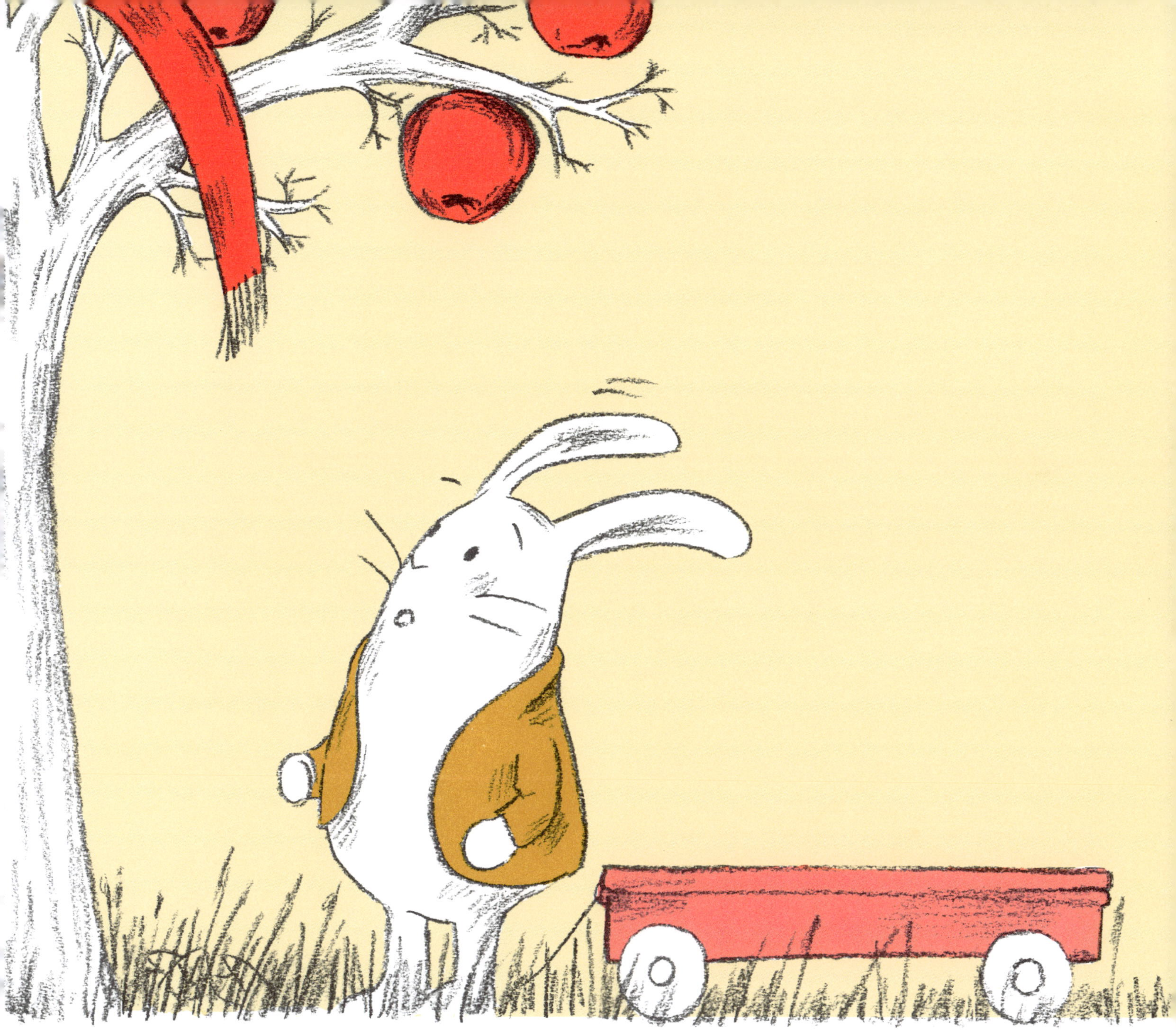

Could you help me

grab

my scarf?

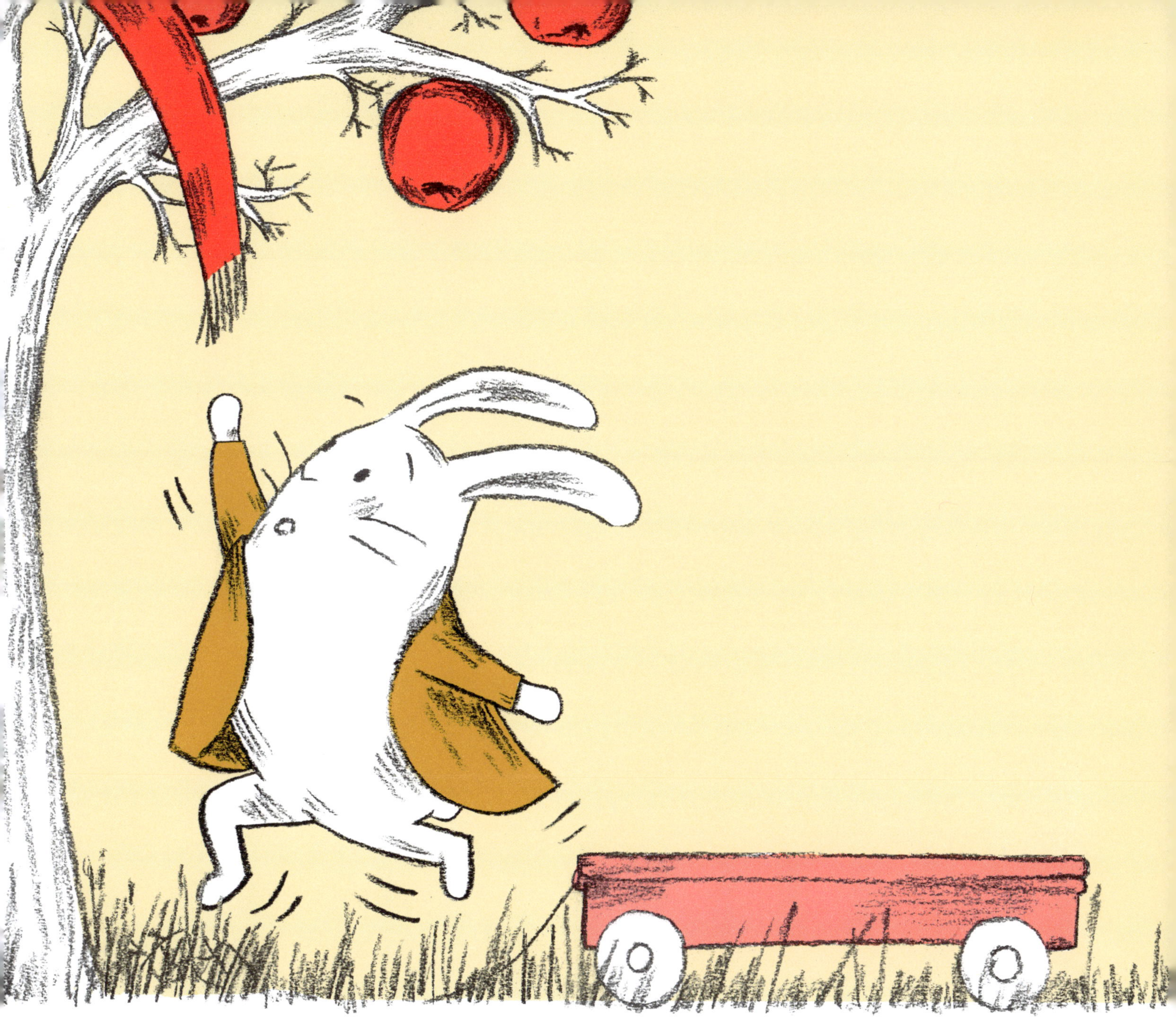

Will you **place** the scarf here for me and **hold** it tight? I can use it to climb the tree and pick those tasty apples!

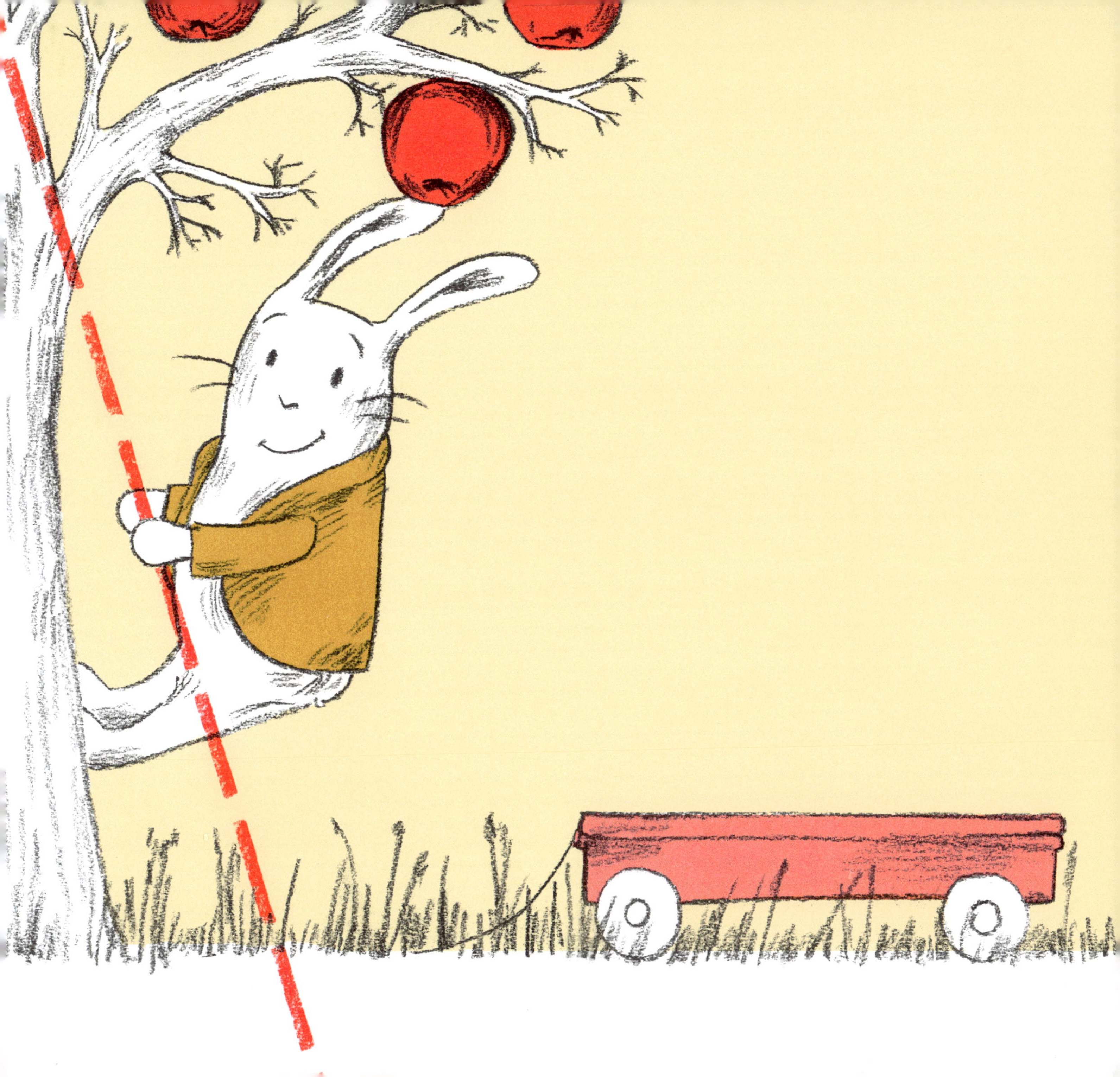

Just one more . . .

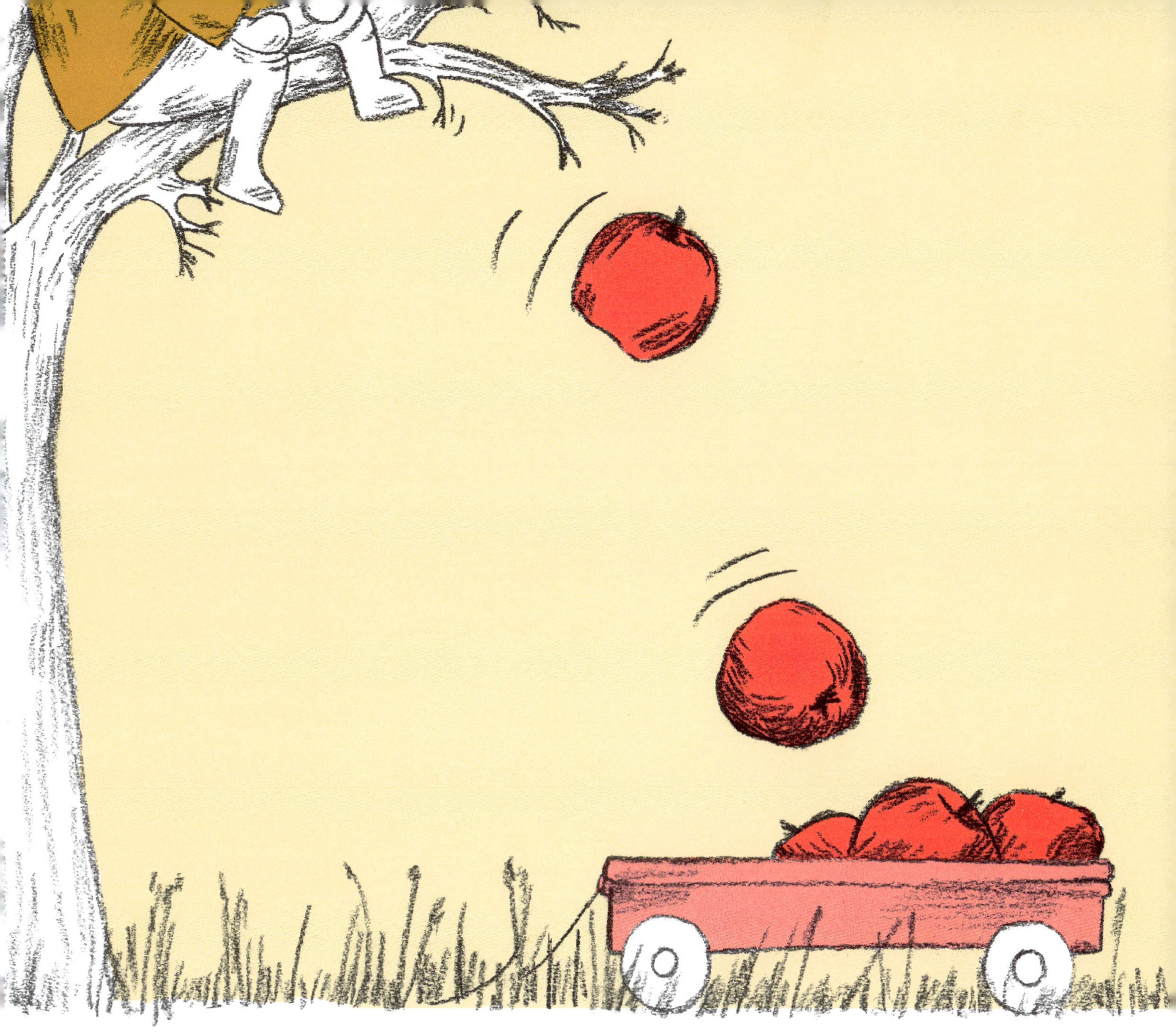

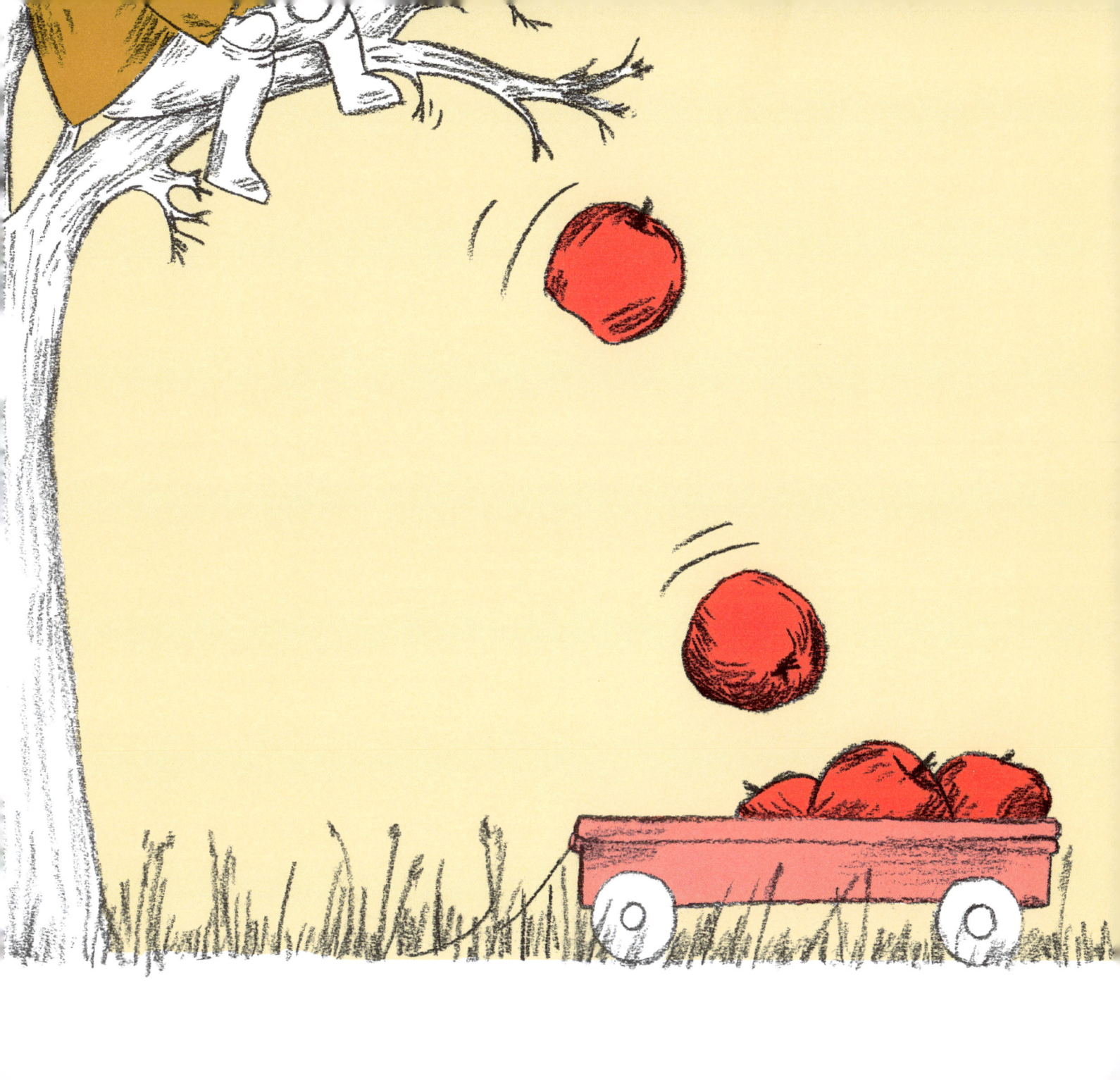

Great teamwork!
I got them all.
Can you hang on to that
scarf for me?

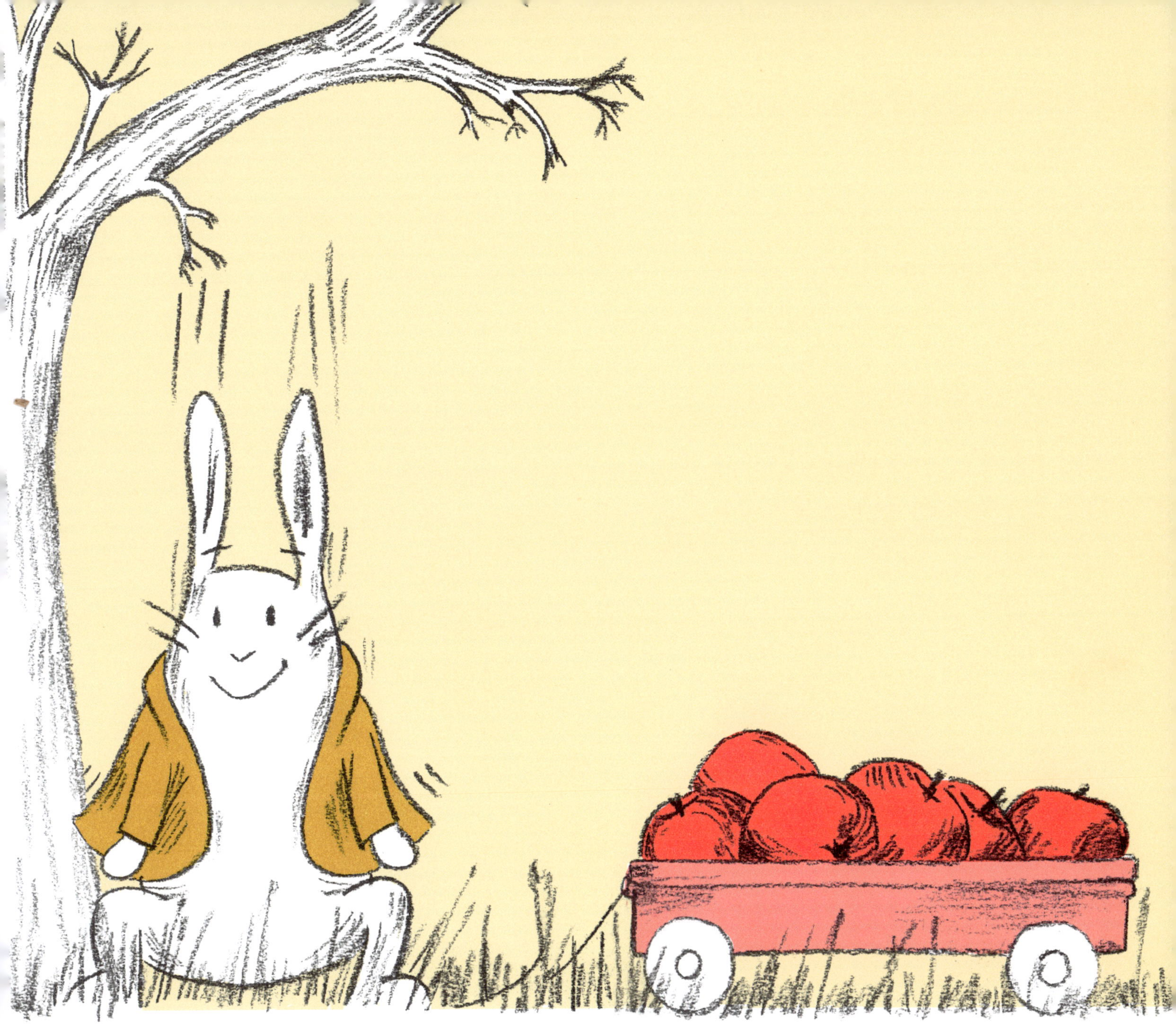

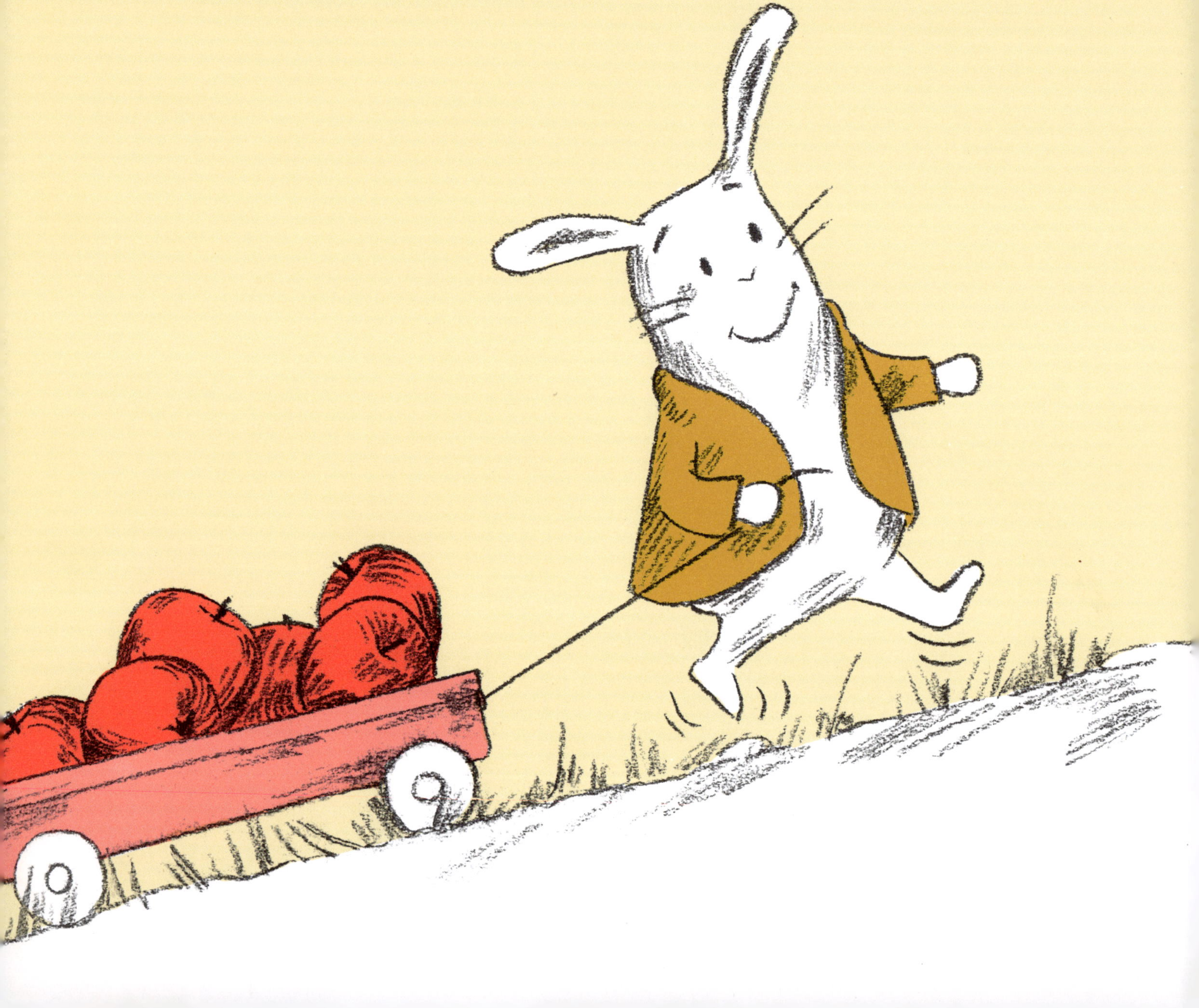

Whoops! I'm running late.
What an uphill battle!

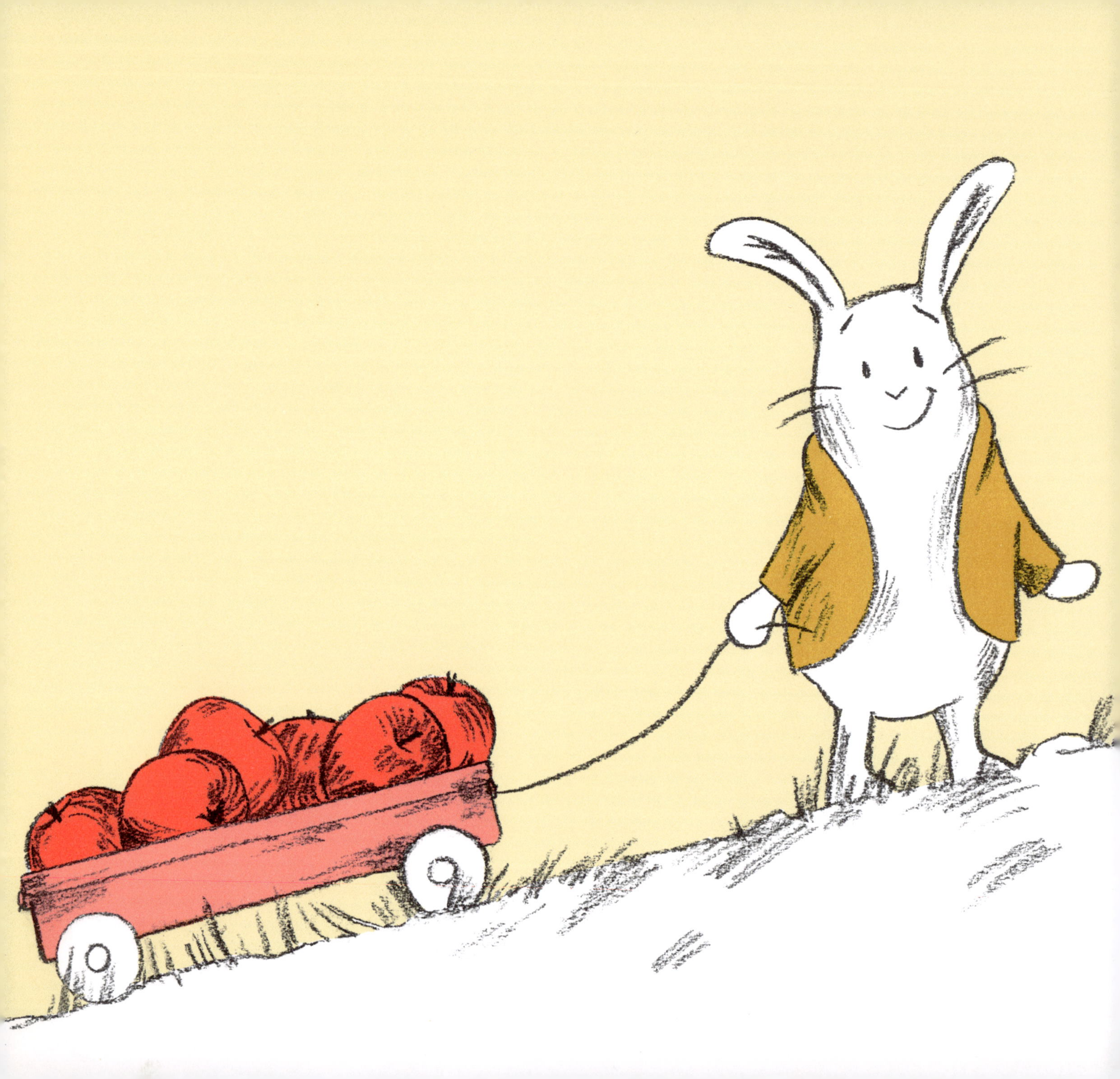

Wait a minute!
Why am I going **up**hill?

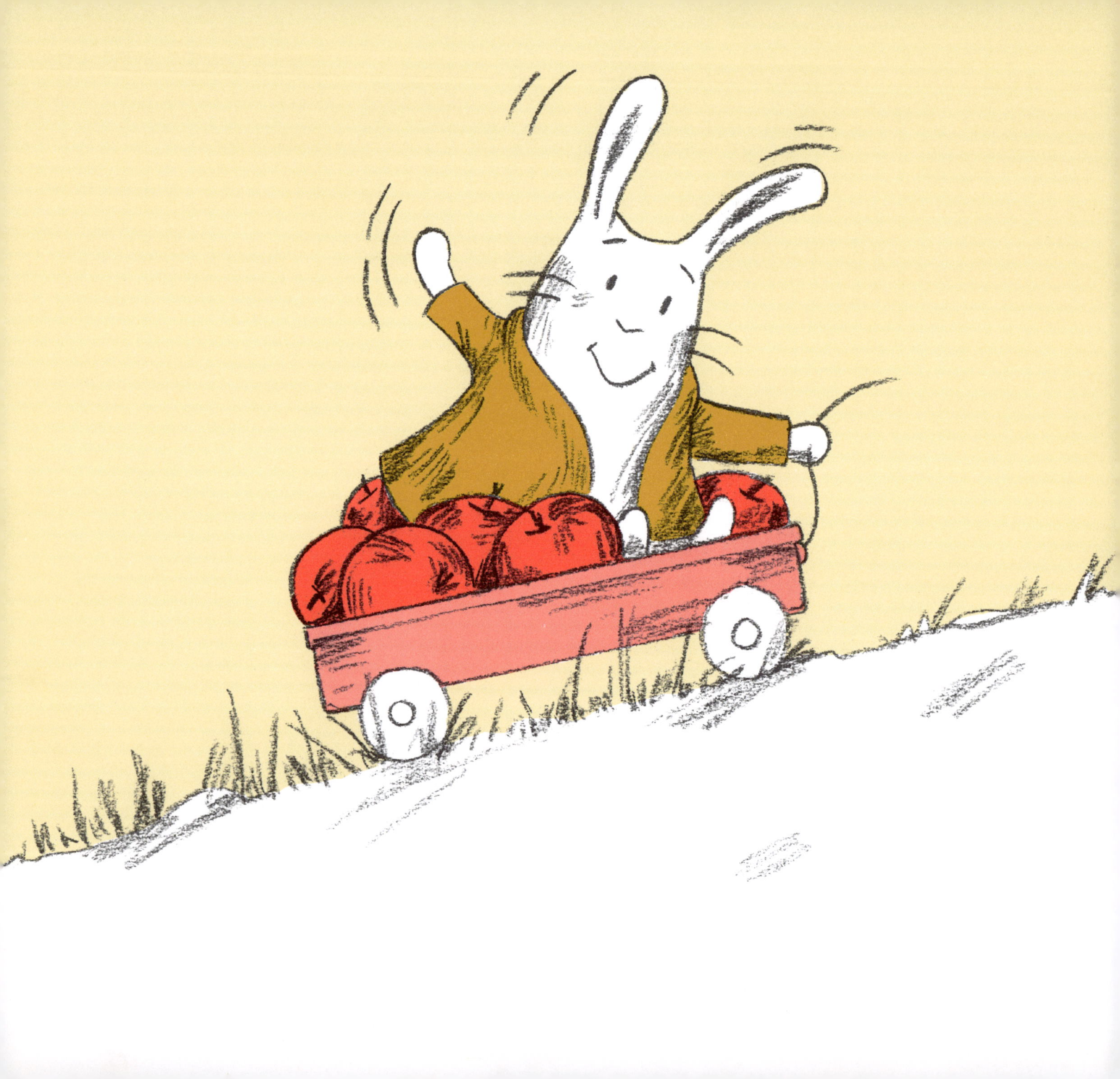

We can fix that.
Can you

tilt

the book for me?

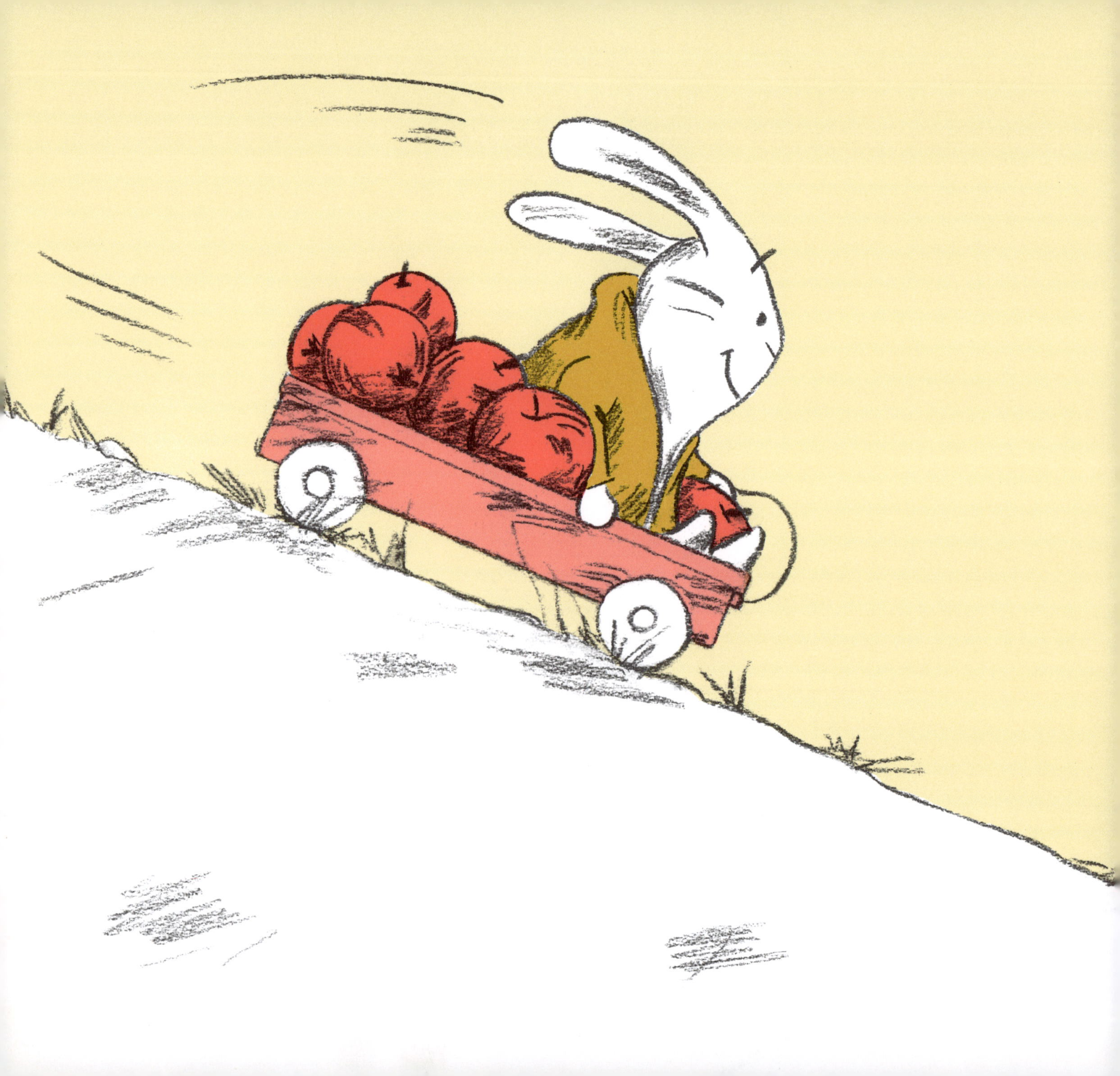

Easy as pie!
Now my wheels are turning.

Why don't we have even more fun?
Would you

rock

the book back and forth?

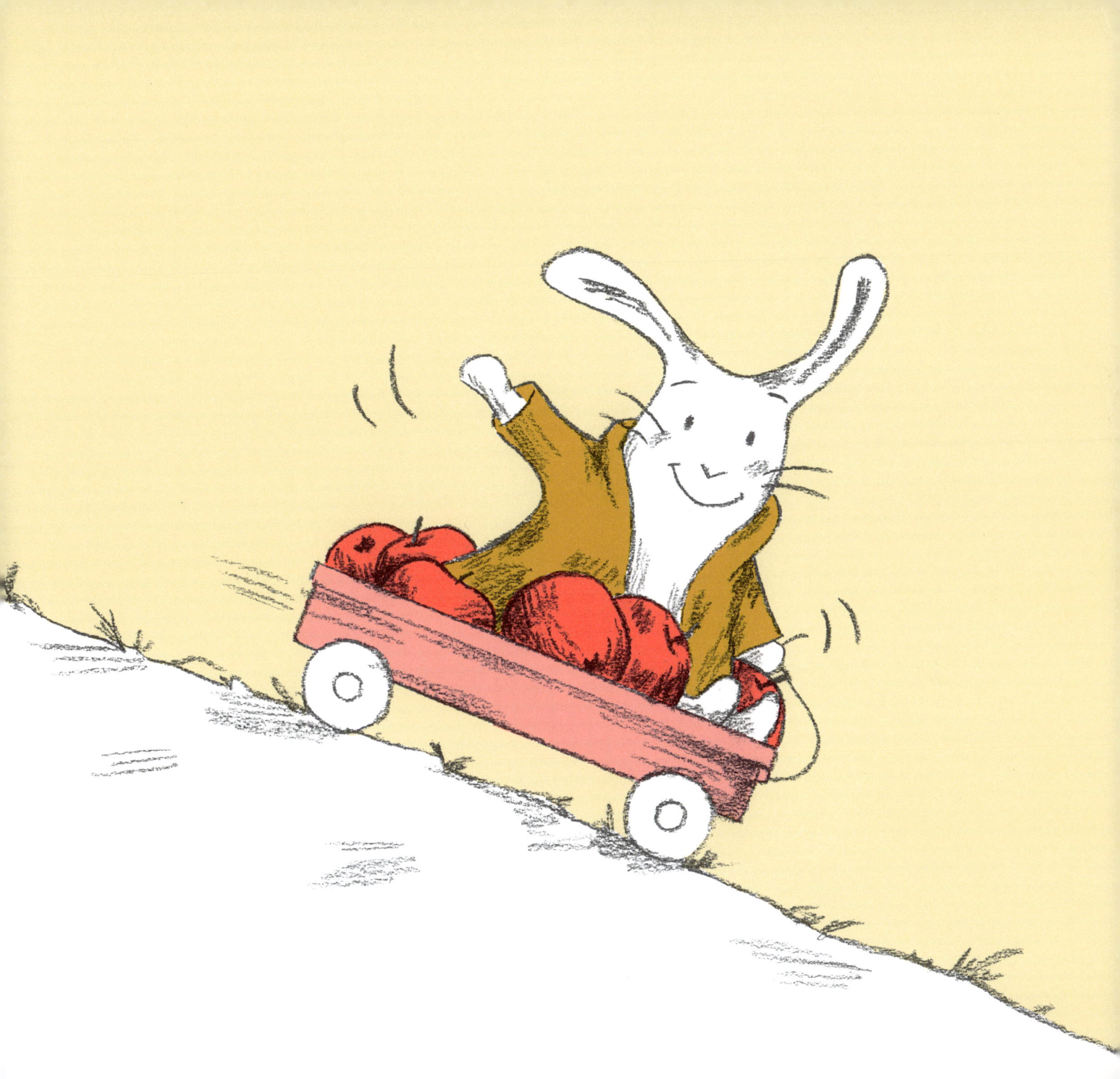

Zowie! Keep going!!

And get ready to . . .

turn!

¡up!

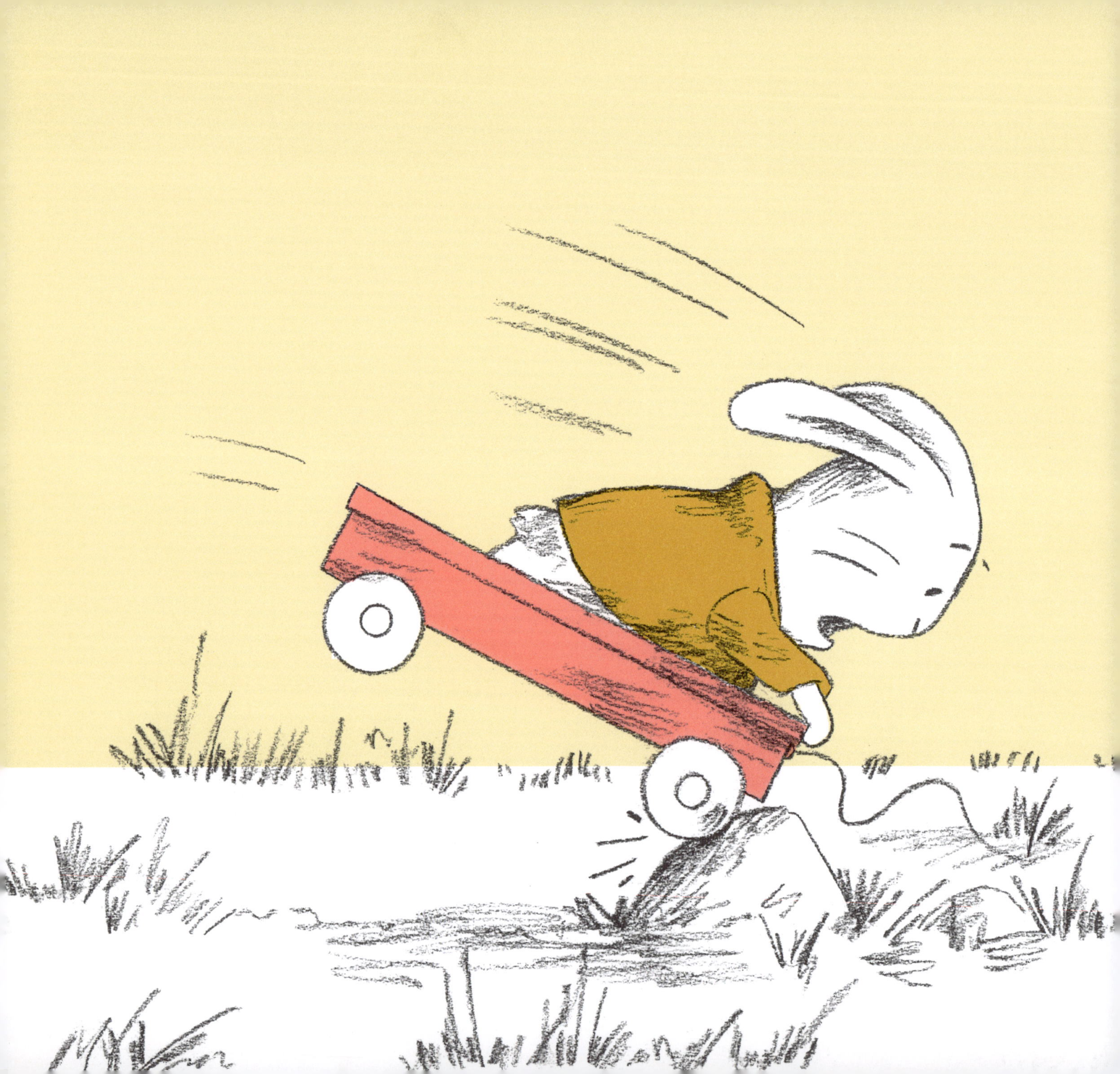

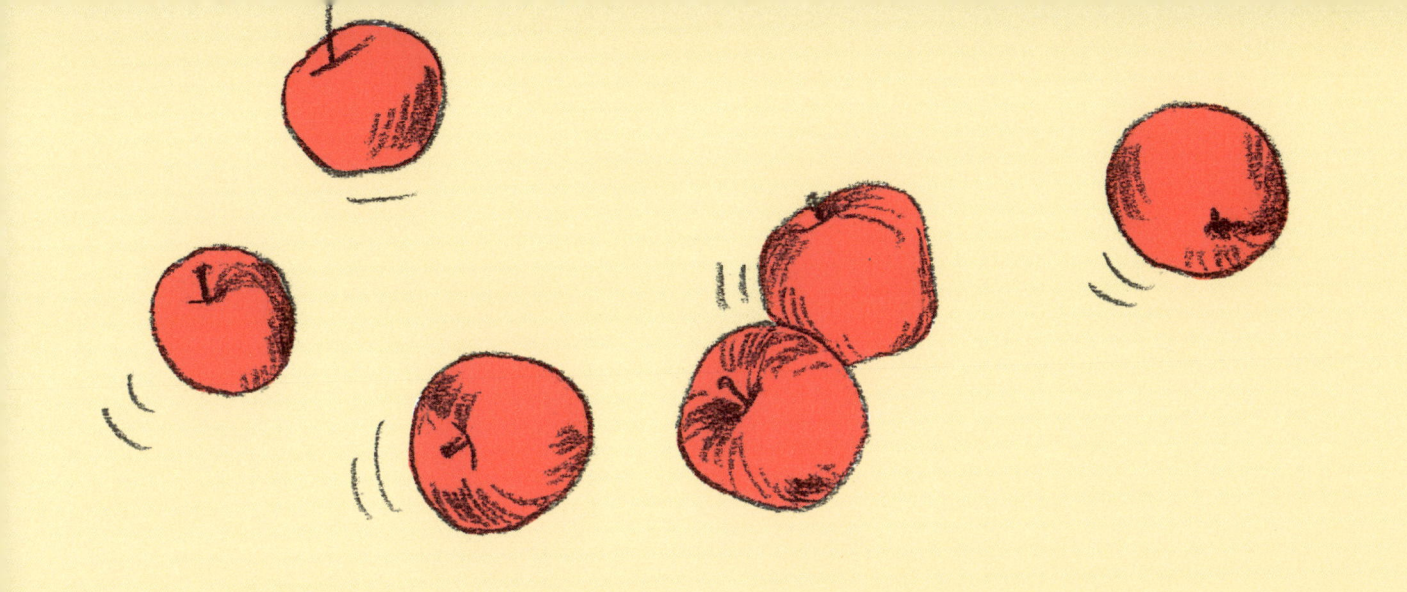

Uh-oh!
Get ready to tumble!

Oops. I guess I upset the apple cart.
Where are all the apples?

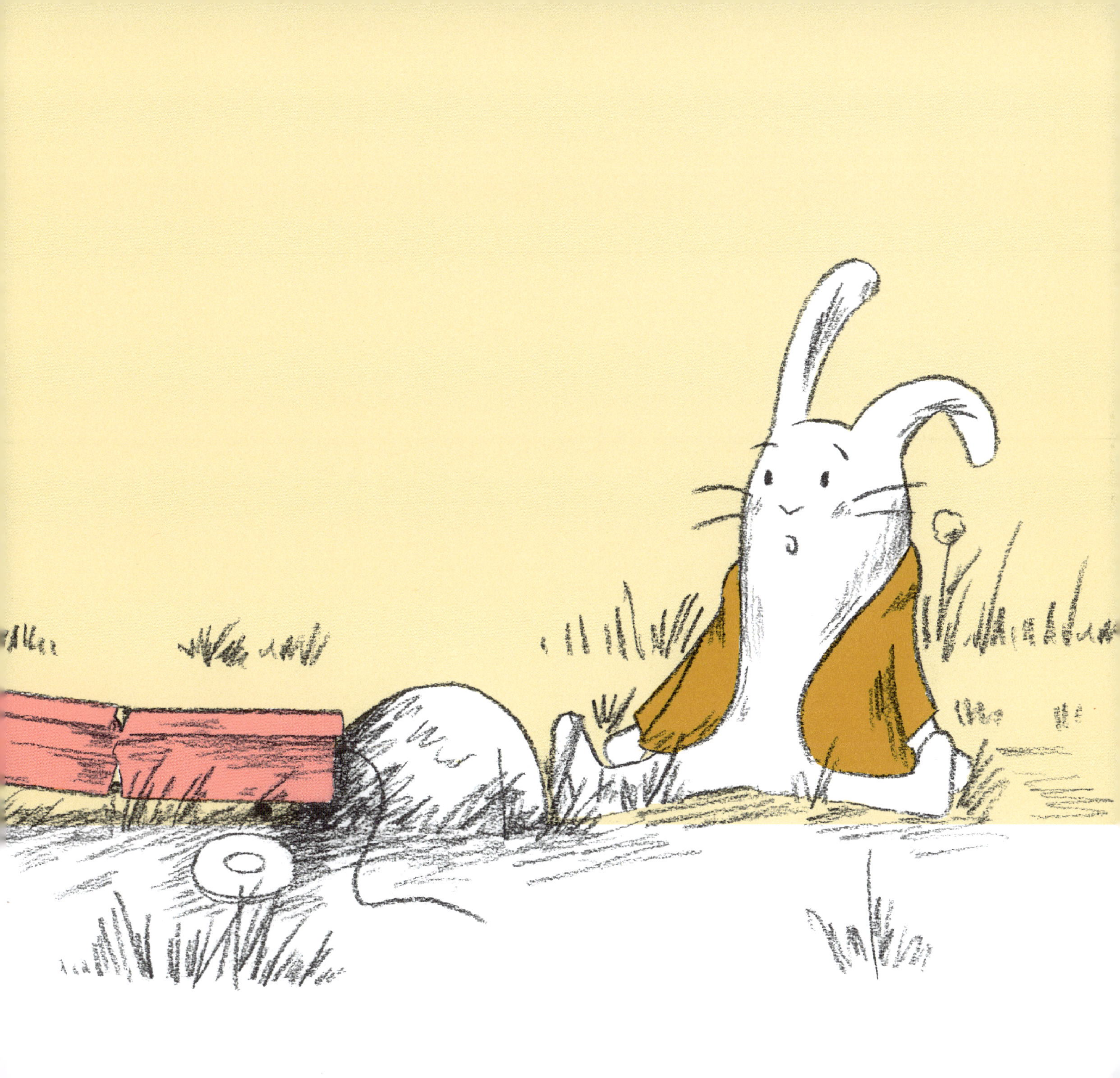

Here they are!
I'll just pick these up.

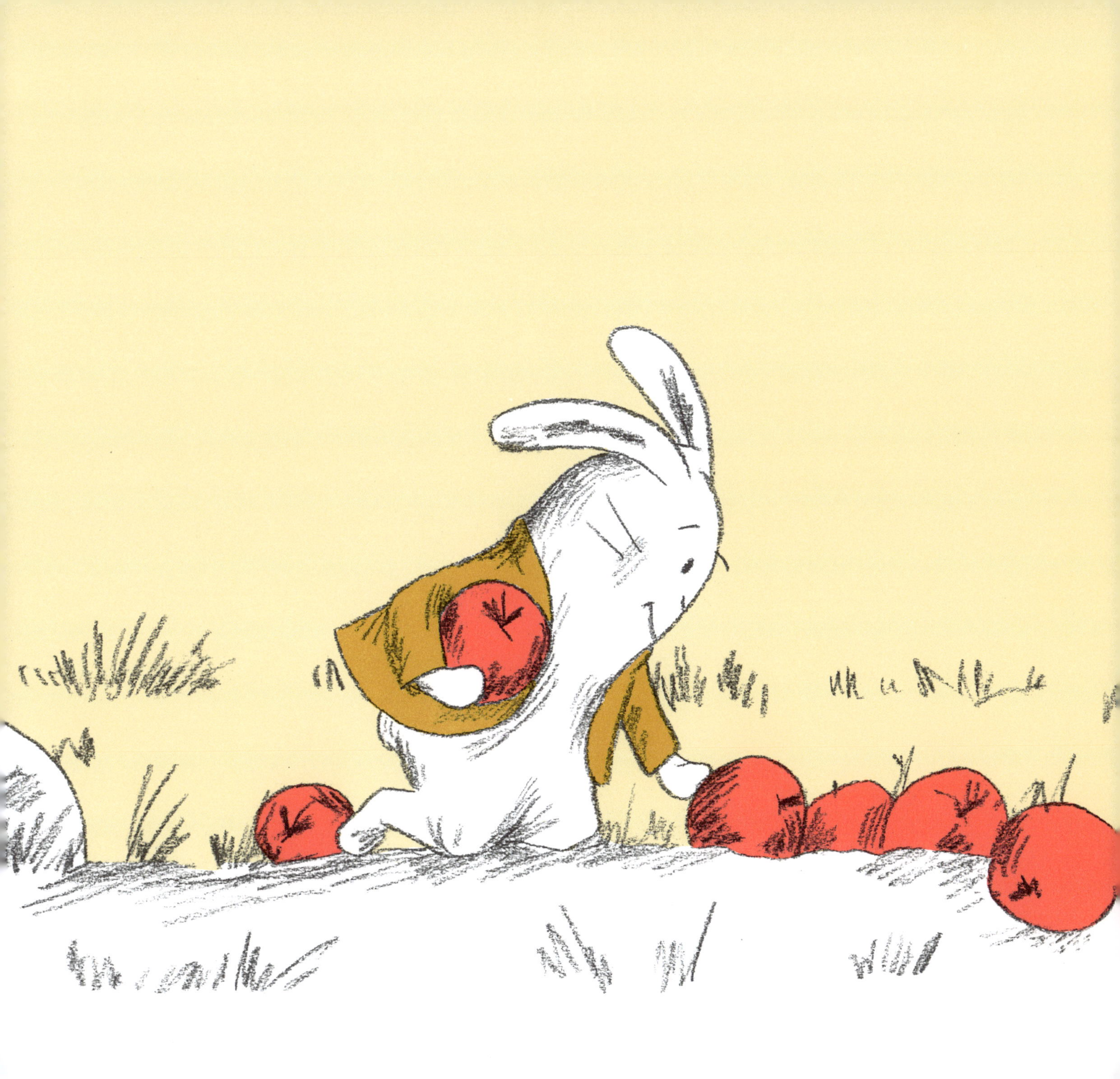

On the road again . . .
but what's this?

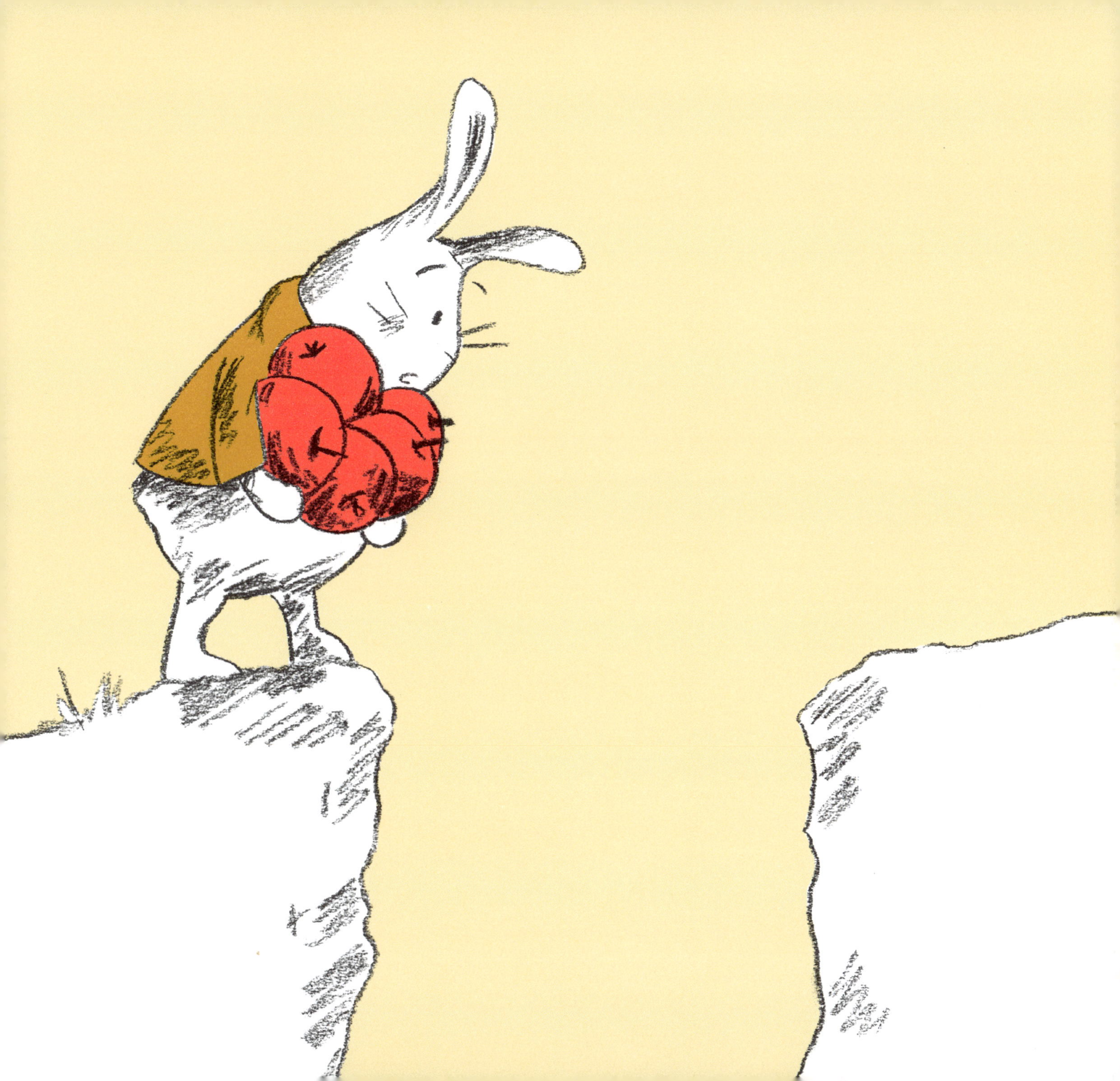

Hey, I think I'm going
to need some help.
Can you use my scarf to

make

a bridge?

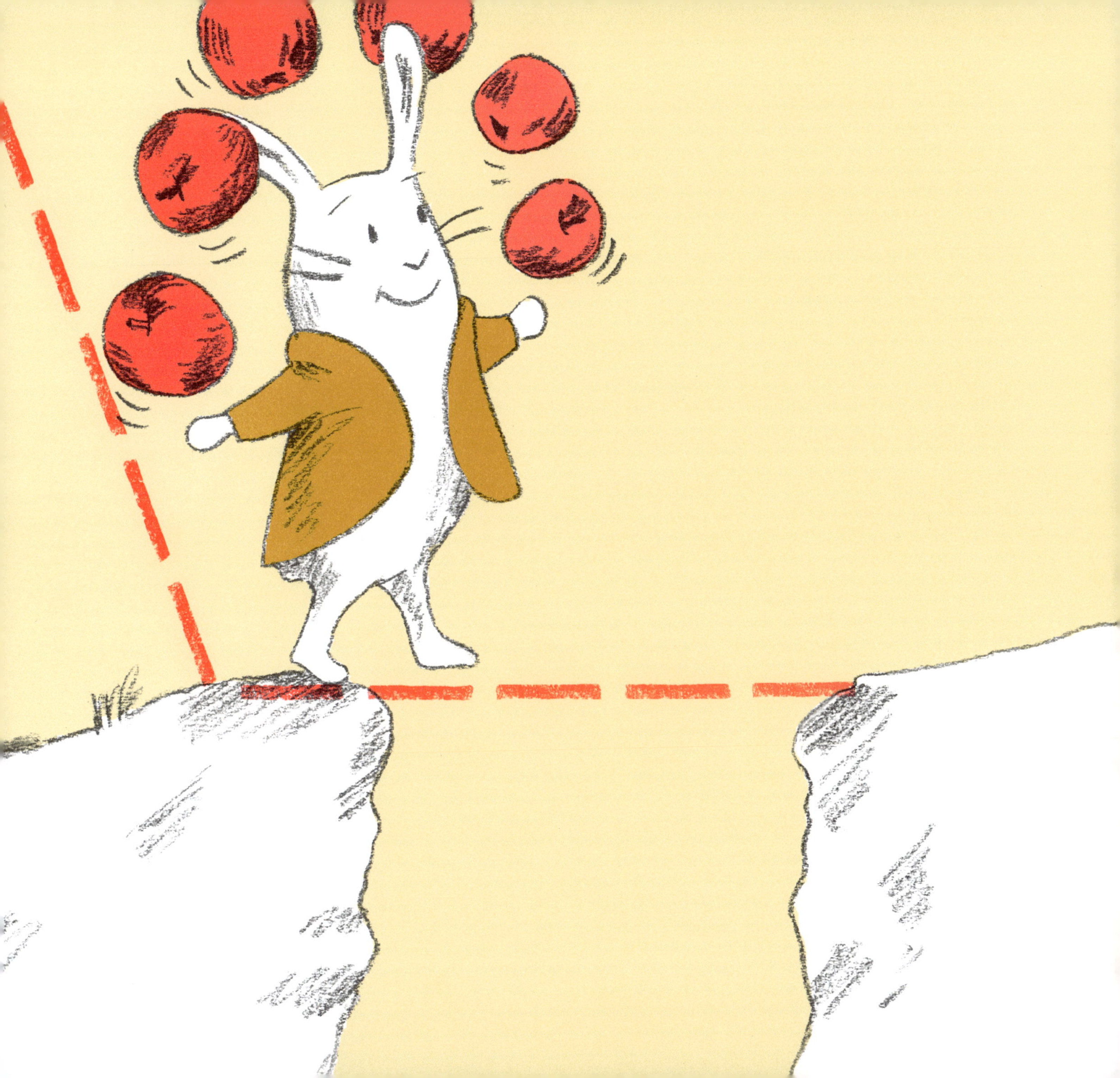

Perfect. Thank you!

I'm at the end of my rope.
Good thing I'm almost home!

Um, I'm stuck.
Would you give me a little

push

please?

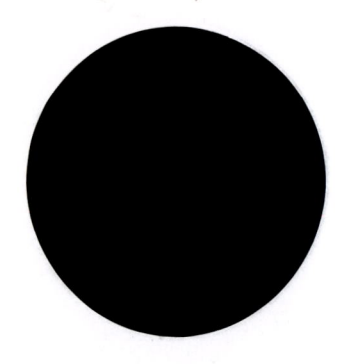

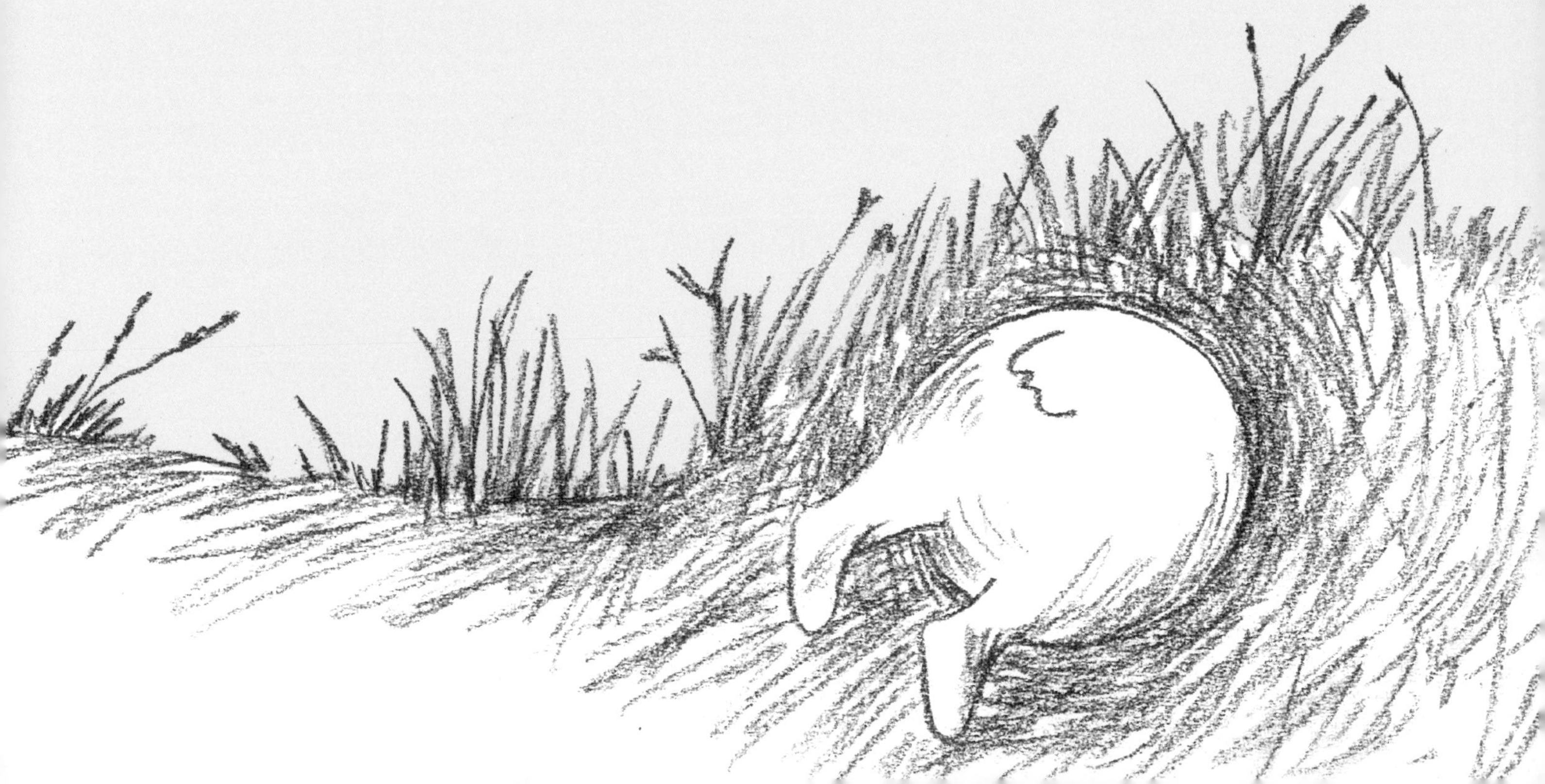

Pop!

Right on time for Mom's apple pie.

Not a bad apple in the bunch.
Yum!

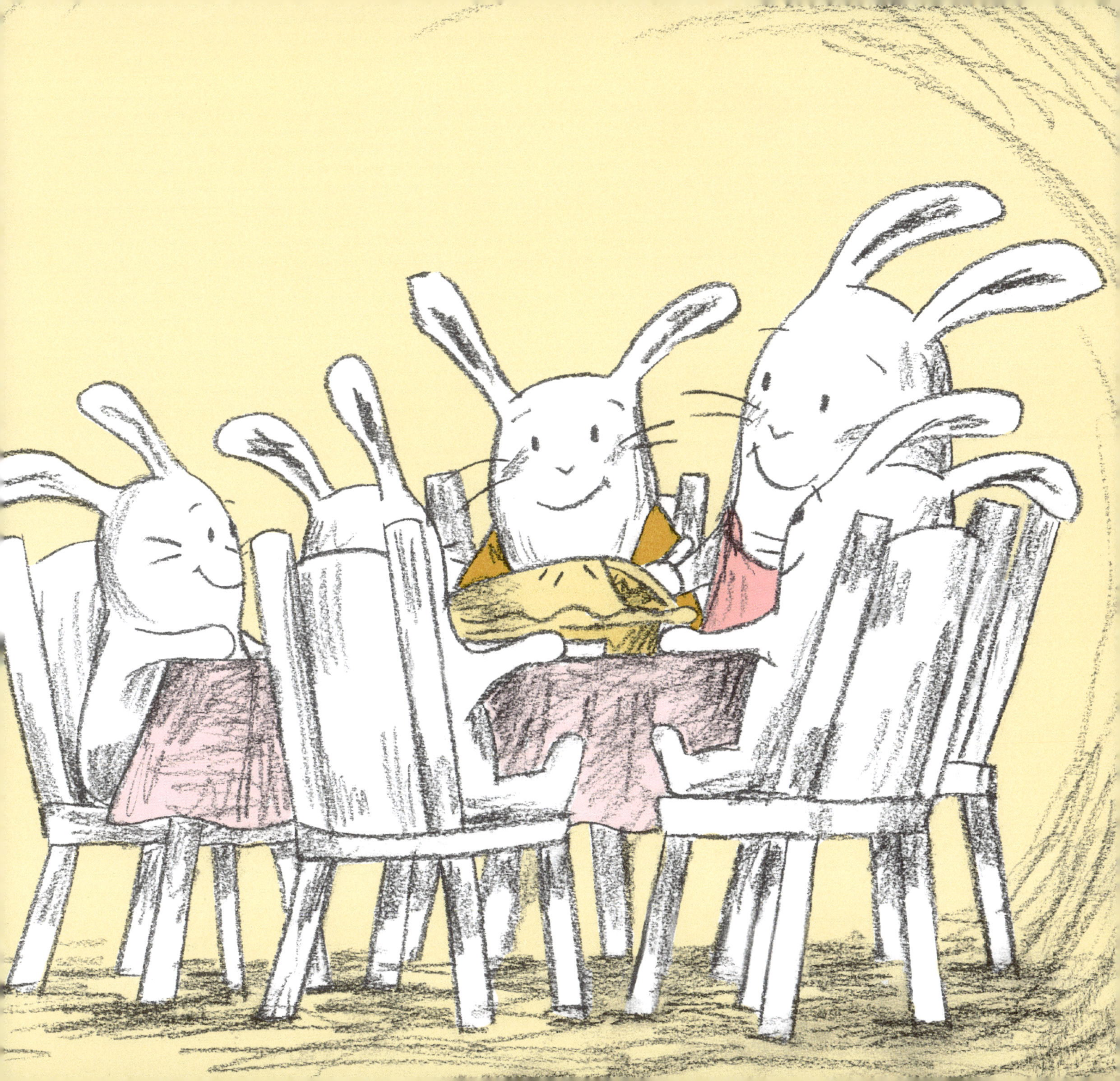

We saved a piece for you.

Bunny would like to dedicate this book to **you**,
for all your help with the harvest.

Also dedicated to children's play.
—Claudia

Copyright © 2018 by Claudia Rueda.
All rights reserved. No part of this book may be reproduced in any form
without written permission from the publisher.

Library of Congress Cataloging-in-Publication Data available.
ISBN 978-1-4521-6255-3

Manufactured in China.

FSC — MIX Paper from responsible sources FSC® C008047

Design by Amelia Mack.
Typeset in Sprout.
The illustrations in this book were rendered in charcoal and digitally.

10 9 8 7 6 5 4 3 2 1

Chronicle Books LLC
680 Second Street
San Francisco, California 94107
www.chroniclekids.com